FIREMAN SAM
AND THE CHEMISTRY SET

story by Diane Wilmer
illustrations by the County Studio

HEINEMANN · LONDON

When naughty Norman Price was given a good school report for the first time, his mother, Dilys, bought him a present – a very expensive chemistry set.

"Now you be careful with it, Norman my lovely," she said. "Use it to improve your brain, no messing about. You hear?"

Norman nodded. "Absolutely, Mam," he said.

He was very good to start with. He kept the chemistry set in his room and experimented with making different colours from vegetable dyes. But that wasn't enough for Norman. He soon started making nasty smells, and then stink bombs and smoke clouds.

"Wowee!" he thought. "I can really have some fun with this!" and one sunny day he set out with mischief in mind.

Pontypandy town centre was quiet that day, so Norman strolled up the hill to the fire station. The first person he saw was Fireman Elvis Cridlington, in the kitchen making lunch for the other firemen. Norman watched him through the window and had his first naughty idea.

"A few of my colours might improve Elvis's cooking," he thought, with a giggle.

Elvis is very proud of his cooking and always tries to make really delicious meals for the firemen. He was busy making something extra special – an Italian meal with home-made pasta.

"Even Bella would be impressed by this," thought Elvis, as he rolled out the pasta dough and cut it into long thin strips. "Fresh pasta made with spinach and eggs. Yum, I can't wait!"

When the water on the stove started to boil, Elvis gently dropped the pasta into the pan.

"Simmer for ten minutes," he said, carefully reading his recipe book. "That just gives me time to mix the salad and set the table. Better get a move on. It's nearly one o'clock."

No sooner had Elvis left the room than naughty Norman sneaked in. "Now's my chance," he giggled and quickly dropped a few blobs of red vegetable dye into the pasta pan. The bubbling water turned pink.

"Oooh, that's really wicked!" thought Norman and he added a few drops of blue dye to the pan. In seconds the pasta had turned bright purple.

"Wow! What a brilliant colour!" he grinned, then he heard voices in the hall. "Help! They're coming back."

"Just come and look at this spinach pasta I've made for you," Elvis was saying. "It's green."

"I'm a bit busy at the moment," answered Fireman Sam.

"It won't take a minute," insisted Elvis.

Norman just managed to scramble through the kitchen window before Elvis walked in with Fireman Sam.

"I've never heard of green pasta," said Fireman Sam.

"Wait 'til you see it," smiled Elvis and he proudly pointed to the pan. "Look."

Fireman Sam stared at the bubbling purple pasta. "It's not green, Elvis," he laughed. "It's purple!"

Elvis gasped. "What?" he cried. "But it was green. I saw it with my own eyes!"

"Well, it's purple now, Elvis," smiled Fireman Sam. "Bright purple."

"Humph!" snorted Elvis. "If I find someone's been messing about with my cooking I'll boil 'em up with beetroots!"

Outside the kitchen window, Norman was listening. He decided not hang around any longer and ran down the road as fast as he could. As he ran, he saw James and Sarah in a field by the stream. James was paddling in the shallow water and Sarah was picking apple blossom.

"Hee! hee!" giggled Norman as he spied on them. "Double trouble here!"

He crept upstream and emptied a whole bottle of vegetable dye into the gushing water. As it bubbled downstream the water turned bright yellow.

"Brill!" chuckled Norman, and hid to watch the fun.

In no time at all he heard a shout.

"Sarah! Sarah!" yelled James. "Come and look at this!"

Sarah dropped her blossom and ran to the stream.
"Oh no!" she cried. "The river's turning yellow!"

"We'd better warn them in the village," said James.

"Hang on," cried Sarah. "I mustn't forget these," and
she quickly gathered up her apple blossom.

As they ran across the fields, James wrinkled his nose.

"POO! There's a terrible pong round here," he said. "It
smells like rotten eggs."

Sarah sniffed. "I can't smell anything, but I have got a bit of a cold."

Neither of them knew that the smell was coming from Sarah's flowers. While their backs were turned, Norman had sprinkled his STINKS bottle over the blossom.

"Hee, hee!" giggled Norman, and he set off down the road for Pontypandy behind Sarah and James.

When the twins reached the village they saw Trevor Evans strolling across the road by the bridge.

"Trevor!" they yelled. "Come and look at this!"

Trevor ambled onto the bridge.

"Quick!" cried Sarah. "It's urgent!"

"Urgent, is it?" smiled Trevor. "What's so urgent, then?"

"The water," gasped James and pointed down at the stream. "It's turned yellow!"

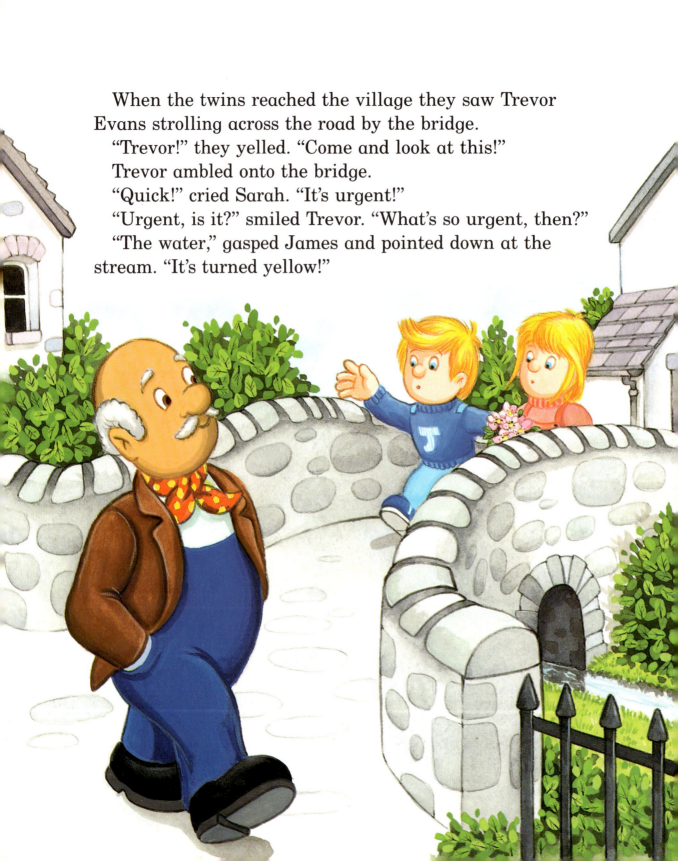

Trevor looked down at the stream and then at James.

"You're teasing me," he laughed. "The water's crystal clear, just like it always is."

The twins stared down at the splashing water. It was clear, as usual.

"What's happened?" cried James. "Where's it gone?"

"You two wouldn't be pulling my leg, would you?" asked Trevor suspiciously.

"No, we're not teasing, honestly!" cried Sarah. "It *was* yellow, up in the field where I picked this blossom." She held the blossom out towards Trevor.

"Phew!" spluttered Trevor. "What a smell! I don't know what mischief you two are up to, but I don't like it one bit!" He turned to go.

"Oh dear, he's really upset," said James, as Trevor disappeared in the direction of Bella's cafe.

"He was very rude about my blossom," sniffed Sarah. "I'm going to give it to Bella. At least she'll appreciate it."

"I wonder what happened to the yellow water?" said James, as he followed Sarah through the village towards Bella's cafe.

"And where did it come from?" wondered Sarah. "It's a mystery."

Norman giggled to himself as he skulked along behind them. "It's not a mystery to me," he sniggered. "Now, what can I do next?"

When the twins walked into Bella's cafe, Trevor looked up from his table by the window. "Watch out, here comes trouble!" he said, but Bella smiled.

"Nice to see you," she said. "Come in, sit down, what do you fancy?"

"I've brought you this blossom," said Sarah.

"Bellissima!" cried Bella. "Please Sarah, put it in some water while I take Trevor's order, OK?"

Trevor ordered beans on toast, while Sarah and James went into the kitchen and filled a vase with water. They didn't see Norman sneaking in through the back door and hiding in the broom cupboard.

"Something smells in here," sniffed James. "It's that rotten egg smell again. Phew, it pongs!"

"Shhh!" hissed Sarah. "Don't let Bella hear you. She'll think you're talking about her cooking!"

Sarah proudly carried the flowers into the cafe and set them on the counter. As soon as she and James had gone, Norman slipped out of the cupboard and crept across to the cooker, where a big pan of beans was bubbling away.

"Now for some more fun," he chuckled and dropped some vegetable dye into the pan. In seconds the beans had turned bright blue.

"Magic!" giggled Norman and quickly dived under the table as Bella bustled in.

But Bella was so busy brewing the tea and singing to herself that she didn't notice the colour of the beans. She just slapped them on the toast and carried them through to Trevor.

"Here you are, Trevor," she said, as she set the plate down in front of him.

"Great, just what I need!" said Trevor hungrily, but when he saw the beans he couldn't believe his eyes. "Blue beans!" he yelled.

"*Blue* beans?" gasped Bella.

"Has beens!" giggled Norman to himself in the kitchen, and he shoved a hanky into his mouth to stop himself from laughing out loud.

A moment later Fireman Sam came in with Elvis.

"Anything to eat, Bella?" asked Fireman Sam. "We're starving!"

"Goodness," said Bella. "What happened to your lunch at the fire station?"

"Something *really weird* happened to it," said Elvis. "It turned purple!"

"Well, I'd skip the beans, if I were you," said Trevor, holding up his plate. "They're blue!"

"What *is* going on?" asked Bella.

"I don't know," said Trevor. "But I reckon it's got something to do with those two."

Everybody turned to look at James and Sarah.

"We haven't done anything," insisted Sarah.

"Of course not," said Bella, giving Sarah a hug. "She's a good girl, look at the beautiful blossom she brought for me. So lovely," and she buried her face in the flowers to sniff their perfume. "Phew!" she cried. "What a stink!"

"I said those two were up to something," said Trevor.

"We're not!" cried James. "And we weren't lying about the stream, either. It really *was* yellow."

"Yellow water, blue beans, purple pasta," said Fireman Sam. "What next?"

"I don't know," said Elvis. "But if I find out that somebody messed about with my pasta, I'll boil 'em up with beetroots!"

As he hid in the kitchen listening, Norman began to feel a bit worried. "Time to go," he thought and made a bolt for the back door. But as he ran he dropped his chemistry set. The bottles went spinning and the powders spilt all over the floor. A big bottle marked SMOKE CLOUD rolled away under Norman's feet.

"Oh no!" squeaked Norman and tried to grab it. But the bottle rolled faster than he could crawl. It hit the wall and broke. All the powder poured out onto the kitchen floor and the pale grey mixture began to bubble and fizz.

"Uh oh!" spluttered Norman. "Better get out of here!" and he tried to reach the back door. But the kitchen was filling with smoke. "Uff! Uff!" choked Norman, and he staggered through the kitchen into the cafe.

"NORMAN!" yelled the twins as he fell into the room, followed by a cloud of smoke.

"What's happening?" said Fireman Sam. "Is there a fire? Everybody out, quick!"

"It's, er, OK, Fireman Sam," coughed Norman. "It's not a fire. It's just a bit of smoke."

"No smoke without fire," said Fireman Sam and he hurried into the kitchen to check.

"Quick Trevor," said Bella. "Take Norman outside. The fresh air will make him feel better."

Trevor helped Norman to the door, but as he walked a little bottle of colour dye fell from Norman's pocket.

"What's this?" asked Trevor, holding up the bottle.

Fireman Sam walked in with a knowing smile on his face. He took the bottle from Trevor's hand and opened it.

"I think I know what this is," he said and poured out a glass of water. "Watch…" and he tipped the dye into the glass. "I think this will answer a few of our questions."

The water turned bright blue. Norman turned white.

"I think we've found the culprit," said Fireman Sam.

"Did you mess about with my pasta?" demanded Elvis.

"Did you colour the stream?" cried James.

"Did you turn my beans blue?" laughed Bella.

"Well, er, yes," admitted Norman.

"What has my Norman been up to now?" asked Dilys, appearing in the door of the cafe. "What's going on?"

Fireman Sam explained the whole story.

"You naughty boy," scolded Dilys when Sam had finished. "But wasn't he clever to do all those things!"

"Clever or not, Bella's kitchen floor is a terrible mess," said Fireman Sam. "I think he should clean it up. Don't you agree, Dilys?"

So Norman followed Bella into the kitchen and started scrubbing the floor.

In the cafe the others grinned at each other.

"After all that, I'm still starving," groaned Elvis. "Have you got anything we could eat, Bella?" he called.

Bella came to the door of the kitchen. "I've some lovely pea-soup in the fridge. I could warm that up. It might just go round." Sarah and James glanced at each other.

"Maybe Norman messed about with that, too!" whispered James.

"Er…Bella," asked Sarah. "What colour is the pea-soup?"

Bella looked at Sarah and laughed. "It's OK Sarah," she said. "It's green. Pea-green!"

"Then I think we'd all love a drop," smiled Fireman Sam.
The soup was delicious.

"Smells good," said Norman peeping through from the
kitchen. "Can I have a rest now? I've nearly finished."

"When you've finished that little job, I've got another
one waiting for you, up at the fire station," said Elvis.

"Oh no," groaned Norman. "What next?"

"Boiling up beetroots," said Elvis, slowly.

Norman nervously followed Elvis and Sam up the hill to the fire station. Sarah and James trailed behind, curious to see what Elvis would do to Norman.

"Right, Norman," said Elvis, pointing to a huge pile of raw beetroots. "I want 'em all scrubbed, ready for boiling."

"What, all of them?" asked Norman, staring at the great pile of purple beetroots.

"All of them," growled Elvis. "Then we'll boil them up!" He noticed Sarah and James peeping through the kitchen window and went outside to see them.

"Are you really going to boil him up with beetroots?" asked Sarah.

"Of course not," laughed Elvis. "But I thought we'd have a bit of revenge. Have you ever scrubbed a pile of beetroots?"

Half an hour later, Norman staggered out. His hands and face were stained bright red from the beetroot juice. Sarah and James burst out laughing.

"Well done, Norman," said Elvis. "Now I think we *all* deserve some refreshments after that. There should be some salad ready for us."

He led the way inside, and a moment later, Fireman
Sam and Station Officer Steele came in. Station Officer
Steele was carrying a large jar.

"Would anyone like a bit of my Doris's pickled
beetroot?" he asked, offering it to Norman.

"No thanks," laughed Norman. "I'm right off beetroot!"

FIREMAN SAM SAYS

Playing with a Chemistry Set can be fun,
if you always follow the instructions.
But never mess around with chemicals of
any kind – they can be very dangerous.

William Heinemann Ltd, Michelin House,
81 Fulham Road, London SW3 6RB

LONDON   MELBOURNE   AUCKLAND

First published 1989 by William Heinemann Ltd
Text copyright © 1989 William Heinemann Ltd
Illustrations copyright © 1989 William Heinemann Ltd
Fireman Sam copyright © 1985 Prism Art & Design Ltd
All rights reserved
Based on the animation series produced by
Bumper Films for S4C – Channel 4 Wales –
and Prism Art & Design Ltd
Original idea by Dave Gingell and Dave Jones,
assisted by Mike Young
Characters created by Rob Lee
ISBN (HB) 434 97318 1   ISBN (PB) 434 97320 3
Printed in Great Britain by Springbourne Press Ltd